To you, Finn and Sawyer—
in homage to your wondrous, marvelous,
and glorious imaginations!

The Almost Fearless Hamilton Squidlegger

Timothy Basil Ering

CANDLEWICK PRESS

During the hours when the sun shares its light, Hamilton is a daring do-*er* and a dream-come-true*r*. Why, he's the rippingest, roaringest Squidlegger in the scrintalberry swamp!

"Dad! Dad! Watch, Dad!" Hamilton calls out. "My mighty shield can block the flames of a fire-breathing frackensnapper!"

"Amazing, Hamilton! Your strength and speed are stupendous," says Dad.

"And my sword can dodge the claws of a skelecragon!"

"What courage you have! It takes one brave Squidlegger to tickle the foot of a bracklesneed!"

One might say Hamilton Squidlegger is fearless.

Well, not quite. He's *almost* fearless. . . .

You see, when the sun disappears behind the scrintalberry
trees, it won't be long before it's . . .

BEDTIME!

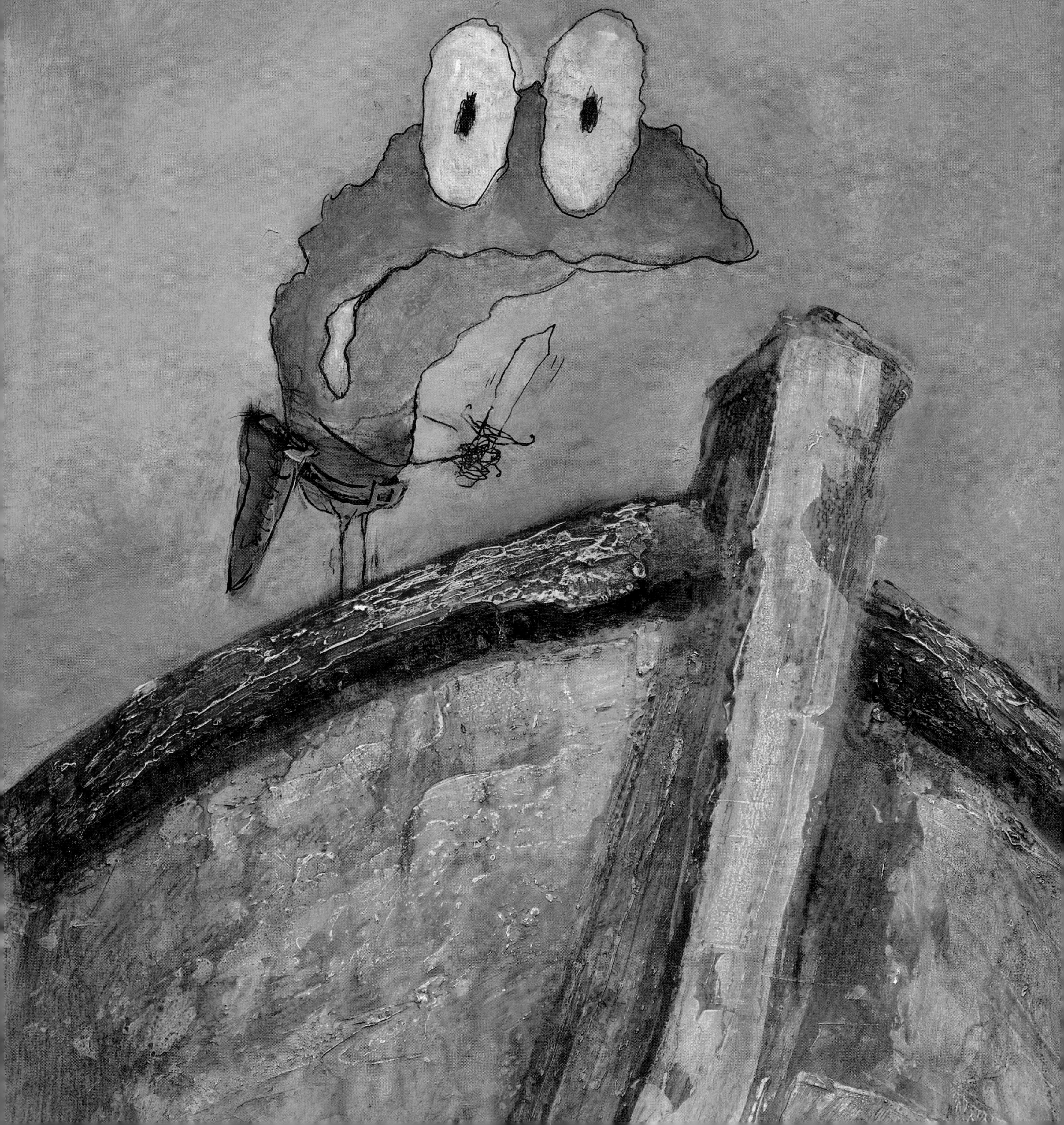

Each night at bedtime, Hamilton's dad has to plead with Hamilton.

"Please, please, *pleeeeeeeease*, son—stay in your own mud tonight," he says.

All alone, Hamilton lasts about two minutes before he hears something. *What's that?*

Is it the sound of a frackensnapper? Or a skelecragon? Or a bracklesneed?

Hamilton springs from his mud . . .

and scrambles to his secret hideaway!

The next day, when the sun snaps up from behind
the scrintalberry trees, Hamilton will wake with vigor.
He is fearless once again!

Well, friends, this went on until one particular afternoon
when Hamilton was sneaking,

wrestling,

and sword fighting,

and his nose discovered the scent of something
that dreams are made of. . . .

A double-decker grasshopper worm-cake, with snake-belly frosting! It was Hamilton's absolute favorite treat.

"I made this especially for you, Hamilton," said his father. "You can eat it *all* for breakfast tomorrow, under one condition: Tonight, you must *stay in your own mud*."

"Anything! Anything for that delicious cake!" Hamilton exclaimed.

But when steel-gray rain clouds darkened the swamp
and the *BOOM* of thunder shook the scrintalberries,
Hamilton had doubts.

he asked, crawling reluctantly into his mud.

"Ha!" scoffed his dad. "What if one does? Think good thoughts is what I say. Monsters are silly, and they love to play! Have a cake fight with it." He gave Hamilton a kiss good night, gently patted him between the eyes, and then doused the light.

Hamilton knew he would be too afraid to have
a cake fight with any lightning monster.

Plus he wanted to *eat* the cake—*yawn!*—
not play with it.

He imagined
licking the
delicious
frosting. . . .

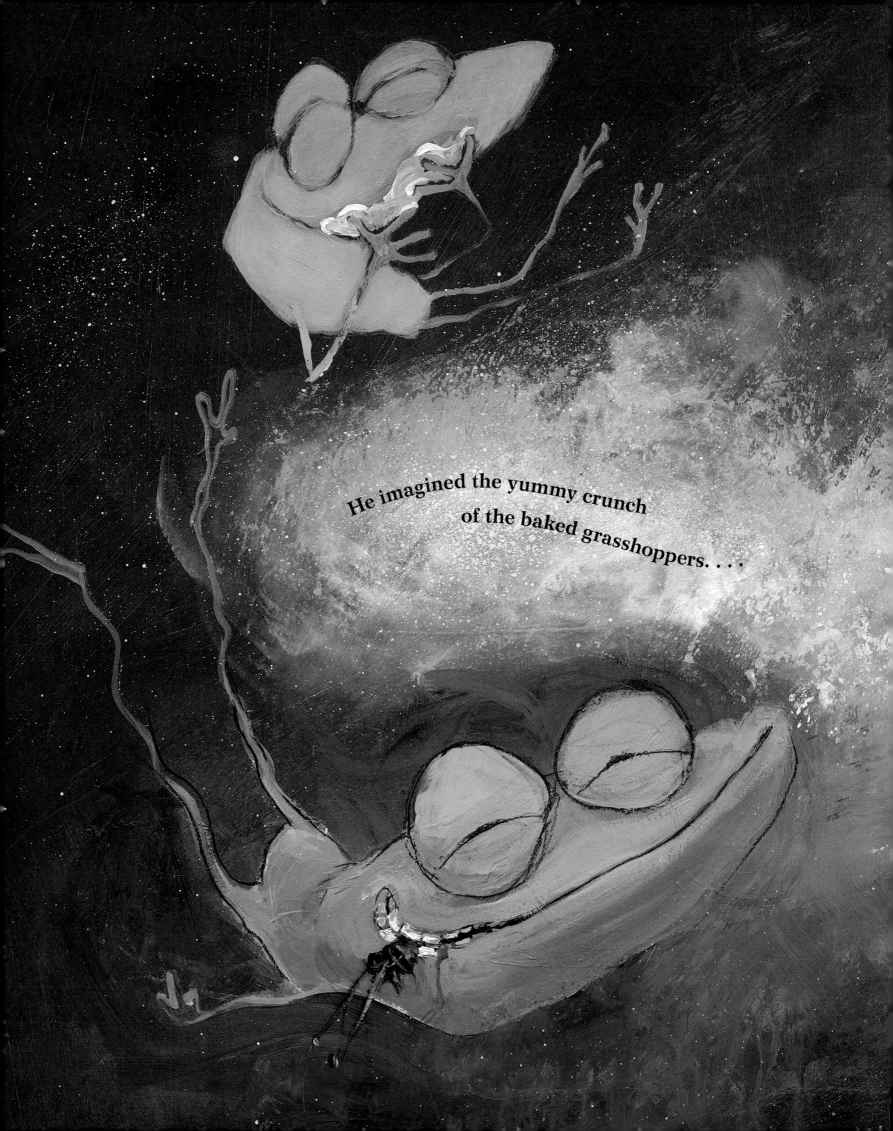

He imagined the yummy crunch
of the baked grasshoppers. . . .

He was a
tongue-length away
from a juicy,
soft-boiled
worm
when . . .

SPLAT! There was a lightning monster!
And his dad was right behind it, throwing a glop of
cake at the monster's ear! Grasshoppers and worms
splattered everywhere as the monster scraped off some
snake-belly frosting and pitched it right back.

Off they ran, giggling and laughing, till they were out of sight. Hamilton followed the trail of frosting.

When the trail ended at an old TV, Hamilton
turned and twisted the knobs. "Where are you, Dad?"
At that very moment, he heard his dad's voice,
and appearing in the TV screen, pedaling a triple-seated
skragencycle, were his dad and the lightning monster.
"Nothing to be afraid of, son, is what I say. Monsters
come because they want to play!"

Then the TV shook wildly as though it were alive, and out from the top, bottom, and sides, a bracklesneed's tentacles appeared and grew bigger and bigger! What's more, the TV was squirting and spraying hundreds of gallons of pink lemonade *everywhere*!

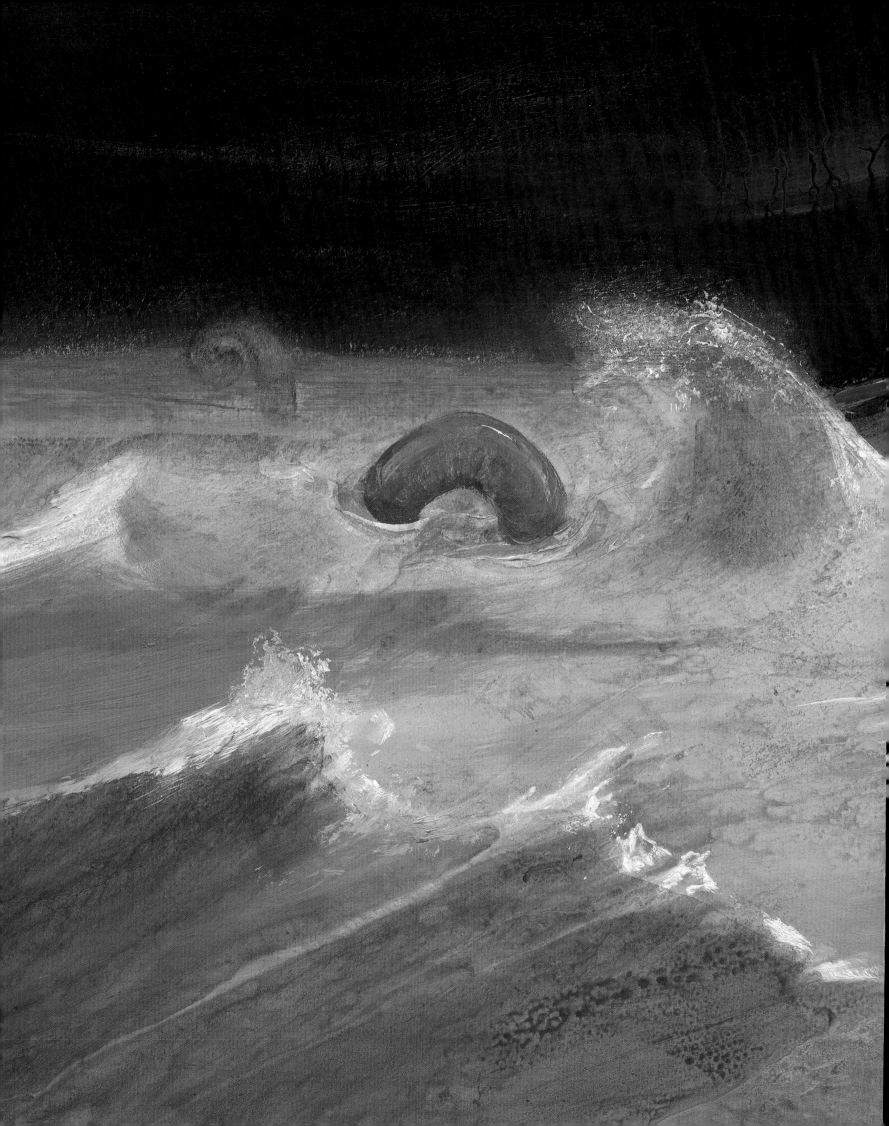

Soon the entire place was flooded. Luckily Hamilton was able to climb aboard a passing ship. But unluckily, the bracklesneed wanted to board the ship, too!

The ship's bow heaved in the huge pink waves, tossing
Hamilton through the air and right down through a hatch
into the galley, where a striped bass stood calmly at a stove,
humming sea shanties and cooking pancakes.

"A monster is trying to sink the ship!" Hamilton screamed.
"No worries, mate!" the bass replied. "I've invited it for a snack. Always be nice to a bracklesneed is what I say. They make great friends, and they love to play." And the fish asked Hamilton to help the bracklesneed into the galley.

Hamilton bravely did as the bass had asked.

"Now to feed my other two friends," the fish
said, flipping some pancakes up through the hatch.
"Upward ho!" he shouted.

Over magnificent and breathtaking things.

But Hamilton missed his dad.

He borrowed a spotting scope and looked far and wide.
Following a rainbow all the way down to where its arc began,
Hamilton saw something that made his eyes widen with joy.

"Dad!" cried Hamilton. "Dad! Dad!"

Who should be on that cloud but his beloved dad and the lightning monster! The ship raced down the arc, and everyone was thrilled to be reunited.

A celebration ensued, and oh, my, could those Squidleggers dance! The friends played and sang together until . . .

the sun began to slip down behind the horizon. Hamilton
climbed back up to the poop deck and gazed out. He knew
he needed to tell the others before it got too late. . . .

"It's bedtime!" Hamilton proclaimed.

All the friends cheered with joy!

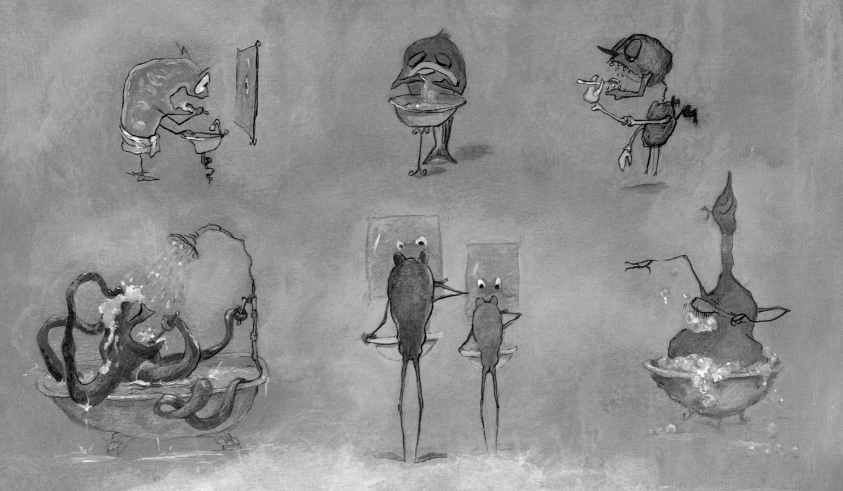

They hurried off to brush their teeth and wash their faces, hands, claws, and tentacles so that they could listen to Hamilton's dad read them a book before they all went to sleep . . .

in their very own cabins.

And that was the moment when the *almost* fearless
Hamilton Squidlegger became *totally* fearless.